W9-DIV-618

UNIVERSITY BOOK CENTER
PI/RF IN
0-688-07888-5 E

DEPT. 2780841014937 PRICE
200 V. OF $14.93

HARVEY POTTER'S
BALLOON FARM

JERDINE
NOLEN

MARK
BUEHNER

to my mother and father
and
to HJ, who once put me on the right track by accident
—JN

to Cara
—MB

Lothrop, Lee & Shepard Books   **New York**

Text copyright © 1989, 1994 by Jerdine Nolen Harold
Illustrations copyright © 1994 by Mark Buehner
All rights reserved. No part of this book may be reproduced or utilized in any form or by any means, electronic or mechanical, including photocopying and recording, or by any information storage and retrieval system, without permission in writing from the Publisher. Inquiries should be addressed to Lothrop, Lee & Shepard Books, a division of William Morrow & Company, Inc., 1350 Avenue of the Americas, New York, New York 10019. Printed in the United States of America.

Originally published in "Never a Worm This Long" by Heath Reading, D. C. Heath & Company. Reprinted by permission.

First Edition 1 2 3 4 5 6 7 8 9 10

Library of Congress Cataloging in Publication Data
Harold, Jerdine Nolen. Harvey Potter's balloon farm / by Jerdine Nolen Harold ;
illustrated by Mark Buehner.
     p.   cm.   Summary: A child ventures out in the middle of the night to see how Harvey Potter grows his wonderful balloons.   ISBN 0-688-07887-7.—ISBN 0-688-07888-5 (lib. bdg.)
[1. Tall tales. 2. Balloons—Fiction. 3. Farm life—Fiction.] I. Buehner, Mark, ill.
II. Title. PZ7.H2312Har 1993 [E]—dc20
                   91-38129 CIP AC

HARVEY POTTER'S

BALLOON FARM

Harvey Potter was a very strange fellow indeed. He was a farmer, but he didn't farm like my daddy did. He farmed a genuine, U.S. Government Inspected Balloon Farm.

No one knew exactly how he did it. Some folks say that it wasn't real—that it was magic. But I know what I saw, and those were real, actual balloons growing out of the plain ole ground!

Harvey Potter had some of the prettiest colors you'd ever want to see on a balloon. Pleasin' Purple, Orange-Ray Sun, Yellin' Yellow. There was Rip-TwoShot Red, and Jelly-Bean Black, Bloomin' Blue, and Grassy Green.

He had all kinds of shapes, too. Round balloons. Long ones. Animal shapes. Clowns with big noses and mouths. He even grew monster balloons with scary faces and great big sharp teeth in time for Halloween.

I tell you, Harvey Potter was a strange fellow all right. To look at him, he was quite plain. Never wore nothin' to draw attention to himself. His hair was kept close cropped to his head. Overalls with a shirt underneath were his uniform. There was nothin' special about his face, either.

What wasn't so plain about him was the conjure stick he carried with him wherever he went. Sometimes he used it to scratch his back, but mostly he just carried it under his arm.

It was Wheezle Mayfield who called the Government on him. So the Government come out to Harvey Potter's balloon farm bright and early one morning. Our whole town turned out for them. And, though nobody said what they thought, we all held our breath hoping we could keep our balloons.

We never knowed how to grow nothin'
but trees—maple, sycamore, pine, oak—
and regular kinds of stuff like corn and
okra and tomatoes. But Harvey Potter
grew balloons. And no one knew what he
used for seed, either.

Anyway, the Government men were standing around in white coats and white hats and white gloves. They kept us so far back we could hardly see, but I climbed right up in the sycamore tree and saw everything.

They pulled and they poked and finally they pricked one of those plants with a pin. And what was supposed to happen did—the balloon popped. Even they couldn't argue with that.

So they gave Harvey Potter the right to grow balloons. He never asked them for it, mind you. But he took it anyway, just to be polite. Let me tell you, it made everybody happy. Well, almost everybody. Wheezle was sore.

Now, I had quite an interest in Harvey Potter's balloon farm. And I decided I was going to get to know him. He didn't seem to mind. In fact, he let me get to know him right good. I'd bring him lemonade, or sit on his porch and swing in his swing, but he never would confide in me about how he grew those balloons. I didn't pry. After a while, I just liked going around him. He didn't ask you no questions about why you weren't this or that. He just let a person be. He let a person sit and think out loud sometimes, and... well...that's a mighty good thing to do.

Still, something in me was a-hankering to know. So I decided I was just going to go out there in the nighttime. That was when he did his field work—I told you he was strange.

To this day, I am indebted to that syca-more tree and to that big ole moon. It was as full as it was wide that night. I saw him the second he opened his door, plain as day.

He stood there on his front porch, hands inside his pockets, looking straight ahead where the fields were. That conjure stick was under his arm. He just stood there, eyes staring straight ahead at something off yonder ways. Then he came down off that porch.

Step, step, step. His steps all seemed so big and so loud—it must have been his heavy field shoes. He walked down to the field and, without a sign of warning, commenced to holler.

The next thing I knew, he started dancing and prancing with that stick held out in front of him, like it was his dancing partner. Then that stick started to glow a nice orangey color and stood up directly on its own. And when it rose up into the air, Harvey Potter rose up right along with it.

The two of them were making some mighty fine footwork, six feet or so off the ground! They were a-floatin' and a-bobbin'. Why, it appeared as if the two of them had turned into glowing balloons themselves! Altogether it was a very strange sight, which got even stranger.

Harvey Potter dropped back down to earth, grabbed hold of that stick, and waved it 'round over his head. He whooped and he hollered and he yelled as he carried on so. "Eeeeeeeeee Ya-Ya-Yayayayaya, EeeeeeeeeeYaYaYaYa."

I am not ashamed to say I was a-mighty scared. I would've jumped right down and run for home, but my eyes were just plain glued to Harvey Potter. Then Harvey let go of that stick and it started to bounce and float over the field, dropping down here and there in nice neat rows. And all the while, Harvey Potter just kept a-whoopin' and a-screechin'. "Eeeeeeeeee Ya-Ya-Yayayaya, EeeeeeeeeYaYaYaYaYaYa!" All of a sudden that stick came to a complete halt and flew right back into his hand.

That's when Harvey Potter stopped screeching. He turned around and looked directly up at that sycamore tree. I thought for sure he saw me. But I guess not, 'cause he turned back on around and went into his house and didn't come out again.

I climbed down and fell off to sleep waiting. In the morning, when I woke up wet with dew and shivering cold, little-bitty colored mounds were popping up all over the ground. When I ran back after suppertime, they had all come up in the glory of that day's sun. I tell you, it was a sight!

Harvey Potter saw me out there in his fields admiring his latest crop of balloons. He said I could take as many as I wanted. I took three. A clown, and an elephant, and I couldn't resist the Jelly-Bean Black one. I didn't touch the monster ones on account of they were too plain scary.

Oh, those were the times! Harvey
Potter went right on growing the best,
prettiest balloons this side of anywhere.
And we never heard a word from the Government men again, either.

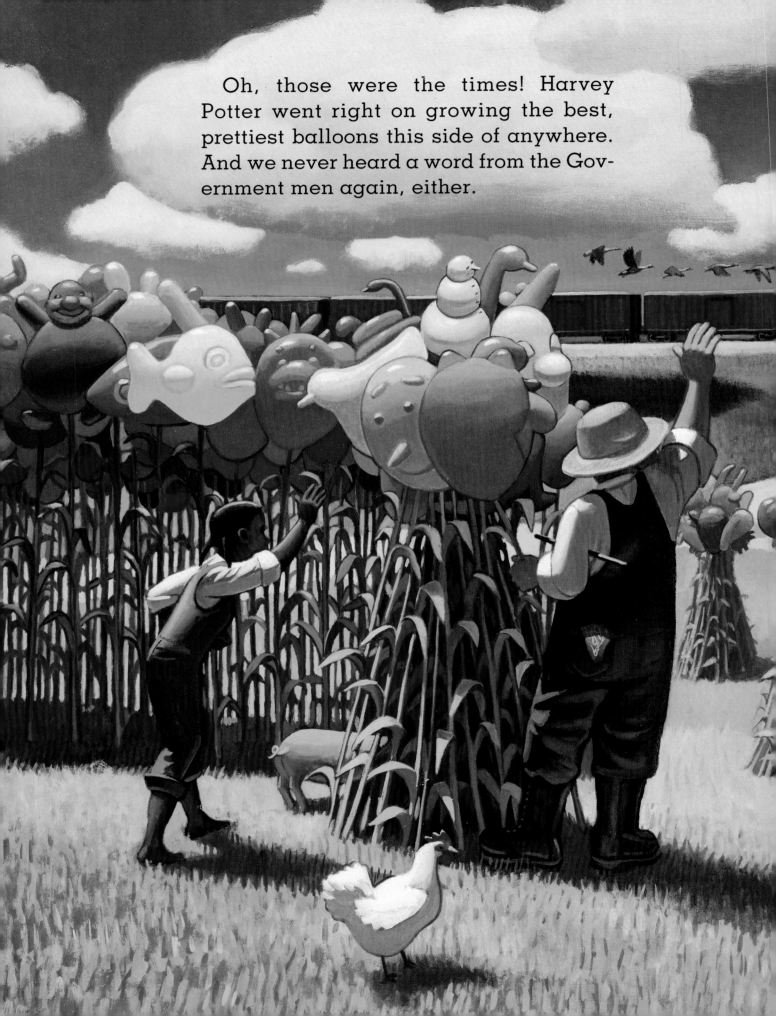

As for Wheezle Mayfield, he was so riled up over the fun we were having with our balloons, he packed up and moved off to parts unknown.

I remember those days well. It was the summer of '29, when I was hankering to leave home myself to find out what the world had to offer. Harvey Potter grew me a balloon that was big enough to carry me off. That's how I landed in this place here. I never did go back home and never did want to. This here place was just right for me.

These days I farm. And I am not one to brag, but I have harvested my thirty-second crop of balloons. Now, I don't grow mine the exact same way as Harvey Potter does on account of I am not Harvey Potter. I have my own methods. Maybe I'll show you someday.